Shoham's Bangle

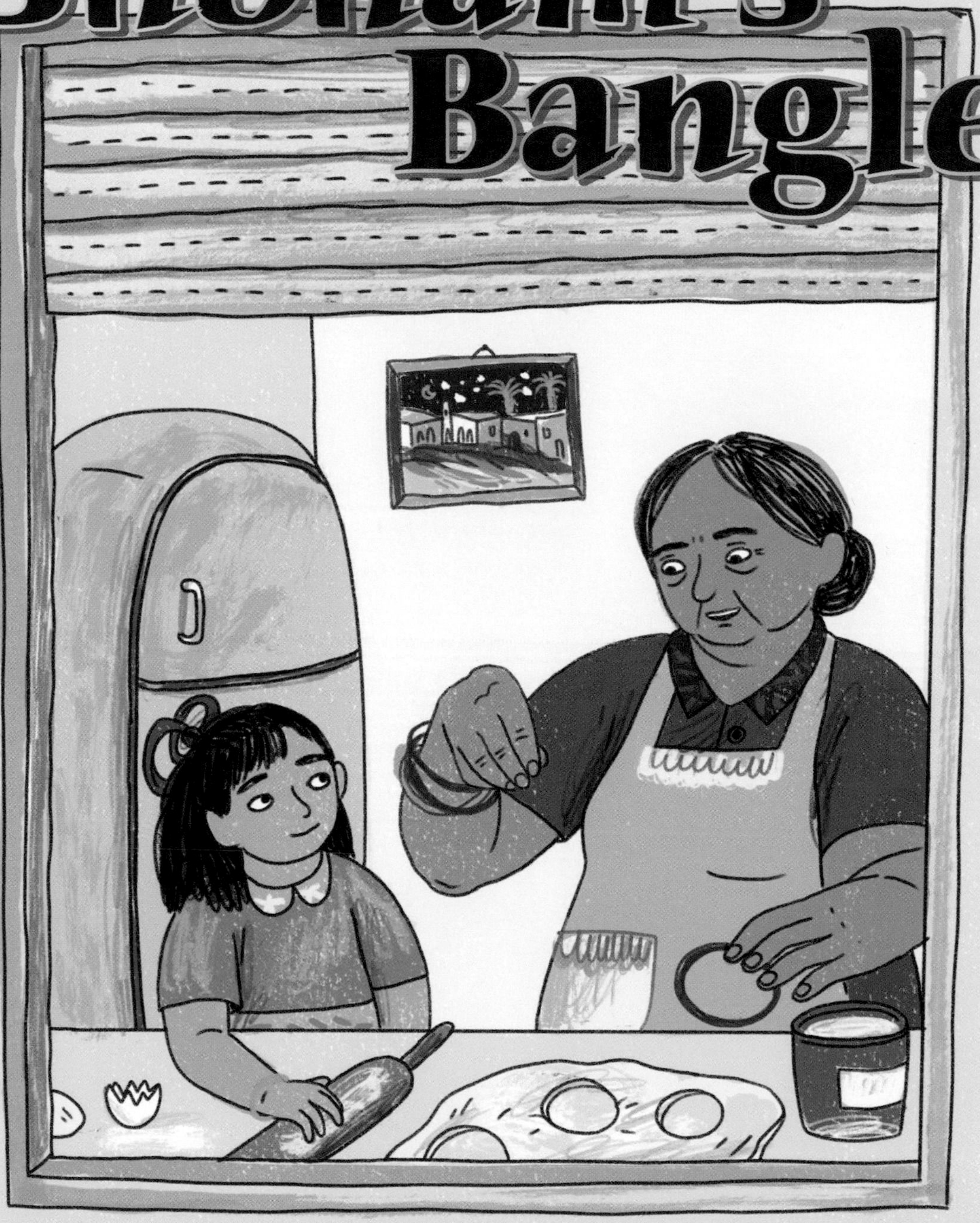

To Nana Aziza, Abba Naji, and their children—
who left Baghdad with one small suitcase and a
lot of heart—who taught me that being together
is what matters. And for David, Eliyahu, Shlomo,
Yosef, and Refael, because you are what matter.

—S.S.

To my grandmothers, who immigrated to Israel
from different sides of the world.

—N.K.

Shoham's Bangle

Sarah Sassoon

illustrated by **Noa Kelner**

KAR-BEN
PUBLISHING

**Nana Aziza and I share a jingle-jangle
of bangles. She has many. I have one.**

Our bangles make clink-clanking music when we
chip-chop garlic and onions.

They cut perfectly round date cookies when we bake.

They glitter golden in the sun when we pick figs from our garden.

Best of all, Nana Aziza has taught me that if I don't want to forget something, I can move my bangle from one wrist to the other—my own special golden reminder.

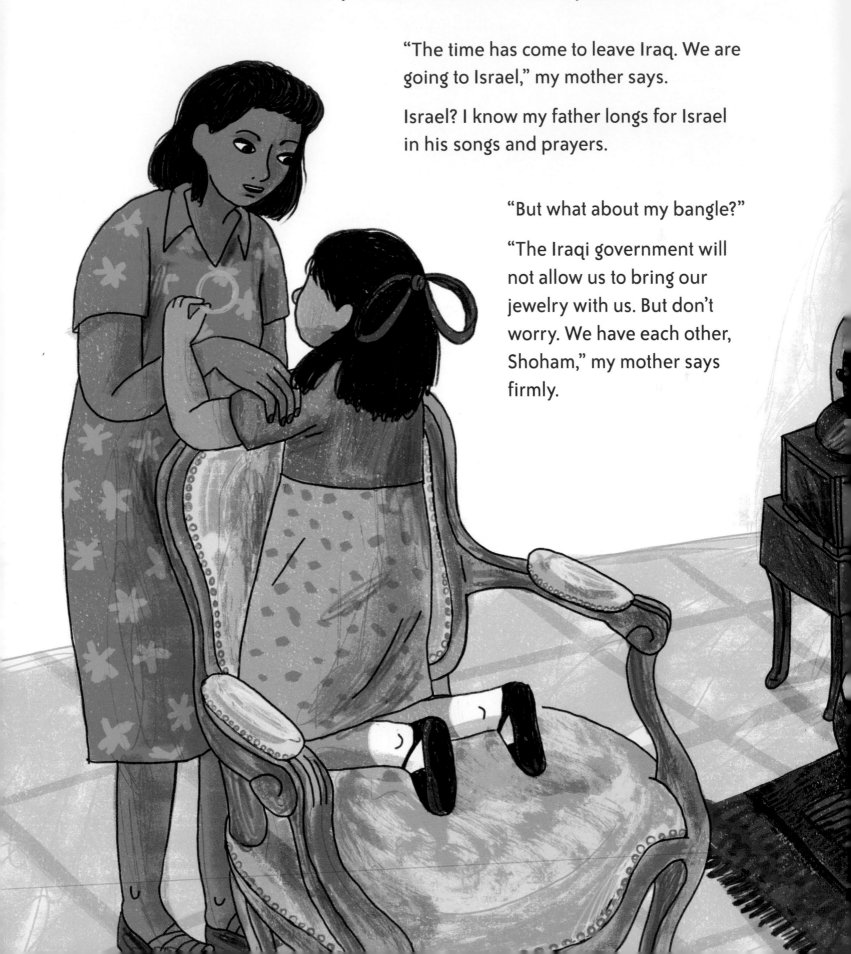

One morning my mother slips my bangle off my wrist, and my whole world slides from my hands.

"The time has come to leave Iraq. We are going to Israel," my mother says.

Israel? I know my father longs for Israel in his songs and prayers.

"But what about my bangle?"

"The Iraqi government will not allow us to bring our jewelry with us. But don't worry. We have each other, Shoham," my mother says firmly.

I don't ask about leaving our house and fig tree.

We are allowed only one suitcase for our whole family: my parents, Nana, myself, and my brothers—M'rad, Baruch, Sabach, and Menashe.

I run to Nana Aziza to check if she knows, to hold her hand, and hear her bangles' music telling me everything will be all right. But Nana is not in her room. She's in the kitchen baking.

Nana holds her floury hands toward me. "The Jewish people left Egypt with matzah. We will leave Baghdad with pita."

Nana's arms are bare, her bangles gone.

She notices my sad face.

"Don't worry. We have each other, Shoham." And she hands me a blue cloth bag, heavy with pita bread.

"Hold this tight, Shoham. Don't lose it, no matter what."

I hold the bag tight. I need to be brave. I will not let the bag go.

The airport is crowded with families hauling their suitcases. We stand tightly packed, like rolled grape leaves in the hot sun. Men and women in uniforms check all the suitcases. Pockets are emptied out. I cling tightly to my cloth bag.

"Open it," the man at the gate commands.

He puts his hand in. I look up at Nana and hold my breath. What if he takes the pita bread away? What will we eat?

I breathe again when the man gives me back the bag and waves us forward.

I hold on to Nana as we climb the metal stairs. We've never been on an airplane before. It's like climbing onto a giant eagle.

The plane is packed, smelly with sweat, and noisy with cries. I touch my wrist—to twist my bangle and comfort myself—but my wrist is empty. I clutch the bag of pita in one hand and Nana's hand in the other.

The airplane roars down the runway, takes off, and soars into the sky.

"We are going to the land of Israel," my father says, his voice bittersweet like etrog jam. My little brothers cry. Someone sings a song from Psalms.

I join the singing as the white clouds surround us like angels' wings.

When my tummy rumbles, I ask Nana, "Can we eat the pita now?"

Nana Aziza smiles. "Not yet. When we arrive in Israel. It won't be long."

It's dark when we land with a bump.

Our parents lead us down the stairs. When our feet touch the ground,
Nana Aziza lets go of my hand, bends down, and kisses the dusty earth.

We ride in an open truck that shakes my bones, until we reach a camp with metal wires around it. I hold my father's hand.

"Don't worry," he tells me. "We have each other."

There are many people, but we manage to find some empty space to settle down.

"We are camping tonight," Nana Aziza says, her smile bright. "On the sand of Israel. The perfect first night in the Holy Land."

The ground is hard. I sit down close to Nana.

"The Israelites slept on the desert floor when they left Egypt," she says. "And now it's time to eat our pita like they ate their matzah."

Finally!

We pass around the pita. I take a small bite.

"Ouch!"

My teeth hit something hard and metal.

Nana laughs.

Carefully, I bite around and around until I uncover my golden bangle.

Nana takes my hand and slips my bangle onto my wrist.

"To remember where we came from, Shoham."

In our new world, I twist and turn my bangle, moving it from wrist to wrist . . .

to remember Hebrew words,

for luck when I play five stones,

and to shape round semolina cookies.

And every night, before I fall asleep, I twist my bangle one last time, to remember our home by the Tigris River where my fig tree still grows.

Author's Note

I grew up baking date cookies with my own Nana Aziza. Her bangles jangled as she rolled *b'ab'eb' tamar* dough flat and shared our family's stories. She related her memories of growing up by the Tigris River in Al-'Uzair, home to the tomb of Ezra the Scribe. She described how she met my grandfather and how they married and moved to Baghdad. And she retold the story of Operation Ezra & Nehemiah, when she was airlifted to Israel in 1951, with my grandfather, their five children, and 120,000 other Iraqi Jews.

Today I wear my own special bangle given to me by my Nana, to remember her and the ancient Jewish Babylonian world she left behind. To remind myself that it's not about the homes we leave, but about the homes we rebuild.

The author's grandparents with their five children in Baghdad in 1951

About the Author
Sarah Sassoon is an Australian-born poet and writer of Iraqi-Jewish descent who grew up drinking her grandmother's cardamom tea. One of her favorite places is in the kitchen, cooking up stories for her husband, four boys, and dog. She lives in Jerusalem.

About the Illustrator
Noa Kelner graduated from the Bezalel Academy of Art and Design. She works with book publishers, newspapers, and magazines, and loves to give stories color and form. She is the cofounder and artistic director of the annual Outline—Illustration and Words festival in Jerusalem and also teaches illustration. She lives in Jerusalem with her husband and two children.

KAR-BEN PUBLISHING®
An imprint of Lerner Publishing Group, Inc.
241 First Avenue North
Minneapolis, MN 55401 USA

Website address: www.karben.com

Main body text set in Bailey Sans ITC Std. Typeface provided by International Typeface Corp.

Library of Congress Cataloging-in-Publication Data

Names: Sassoon, Sarah, 1981– author. | Kelner, Noa, illustrator.
Title: Shoham's bangle / Sarah Sassoon ; illustrated by Noa Kelner.
Description: Minneapolis, MN : Kar-Ben Publishing, [2022] | Audience: Ages 5–9. | Audience: Grades 2–3. | Summary: "When Shoham's family emigrates from Iraq to Israel, Nana Aziza gives Shoham a way to remember where she came from"— Provided by publisher.
Identifiers: LCCN 2021044147 (print) | LCCN 2021044148 (ebook) | ISBN 9781728438962 (hardcover) | ISBN 9781728439020 (pbk.) | ISBN 9781728461090 (eb pdf)
Subjects: CYAC: Emigration and immigration—Fiction. | Jews—Israel—Fiction. | Family life—Fiction. | Iraq—Fiction. | Israel—Fiction. | LCGFT: Picture books.
Classification: LCC PZ7.1.S26478 Sh 2022 (print) | LCC PZ7.1.S26478 (ebook) | DDC [E]—dc23

LC record available at https://lccn.loc.gov/2021044147
LC ebook record available at https://lccn.loc.gov/2021044148

Manufactured in the United States of America
1-49733-49636-1/19/2022